# IT'S TIME TO SLEEP, YOU CRAZY SHEEP!

Alison Ritchie   illustrated by Cornelia Haas

LITTLE TIGER PRESS
London

To Lucy and Jonny ~ A R

For my parents Erich and Heide Haas ~ C H

LITTLE TIGER PRESS
An imprint of Magi Publications
1 The Coda Centre, 189 Munster Road, London SW6 6AW
www.littletigerpress.com

First published in Great Britain 2008

Text copyright © Alison Ritchie 2008
Illustrations copyright © Cornelia Haas 2008
Alison Ritchie and Cornelia Haas have asserted their rights
to be identified as the author and illustrator of this work
under the Copyright, Designs and Patents Act, 1988

A CIP catalogue record for this book is available
from the British Library

Printed in Singapore

10 9 8 7 6 5 4 3 2 1

Tucked up tight, all warm and snug,
Phoebe tries to sleep.
She shuts her eyes, but she's not tired:
she needs to count her sheep!

But Phoebe's sheep have other plans –
they're bored of jumping gates.
They're heading for the ice rink,
and putting on their skates.

They slip and slide, they zip and glide,
their feet a tangled blur.
They skim along the frozen ice,
like fluffy balls of fur.

Now they're revving up their bikes.
They like to travel fast!

"Wait!" cries Phoebe, but her sheep just wave as they whizz past.

They've reached the highest cliff top now.
"Come **back** here!" Phoebe begs.
But off they fly into the sky,
to float like clouds on legs.

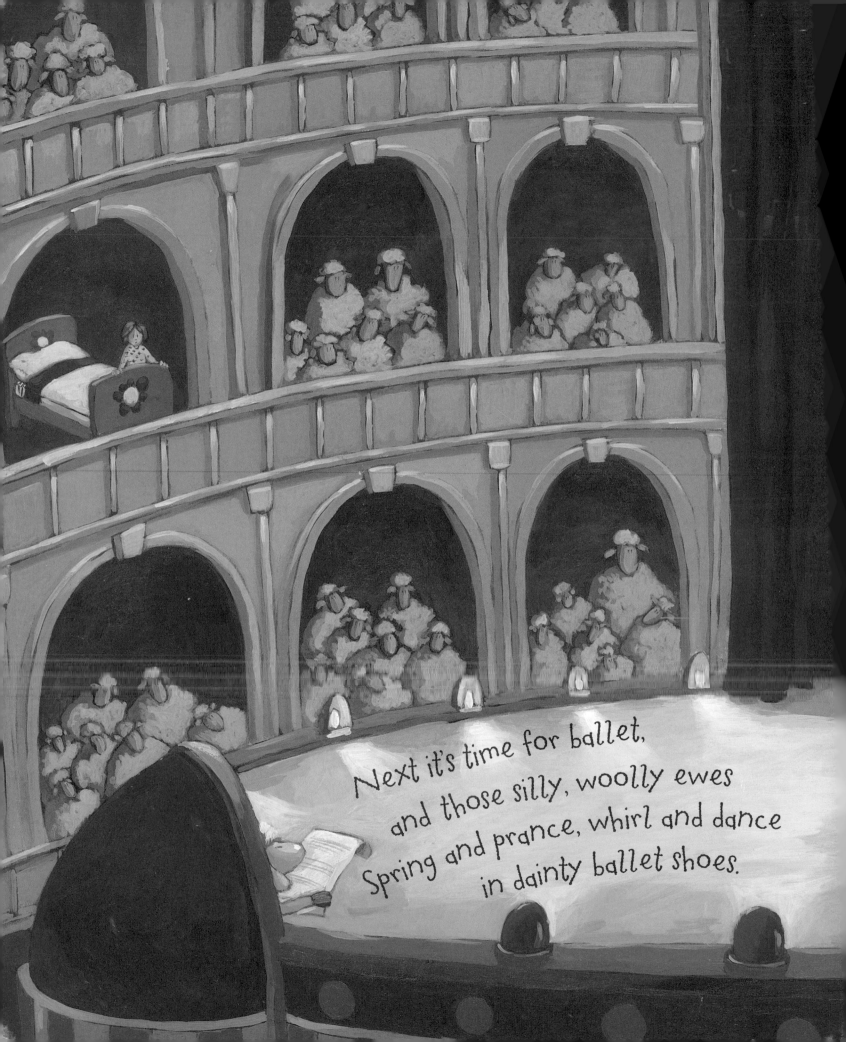

Next it's time for ballet,
and those silly, woolly ewes
spring and prance, whirl and dance
in dainty ballet shoes.

"Stop it, stop it!" Phoebe wails.
"Let me count you, please!"
But her sheep zoom down the slope,
Zig-zagging through the trees.

BoING!

Bouncing on a trampoline,
up and down they go.
Like daring circus acrobats,
they're putting on a show!

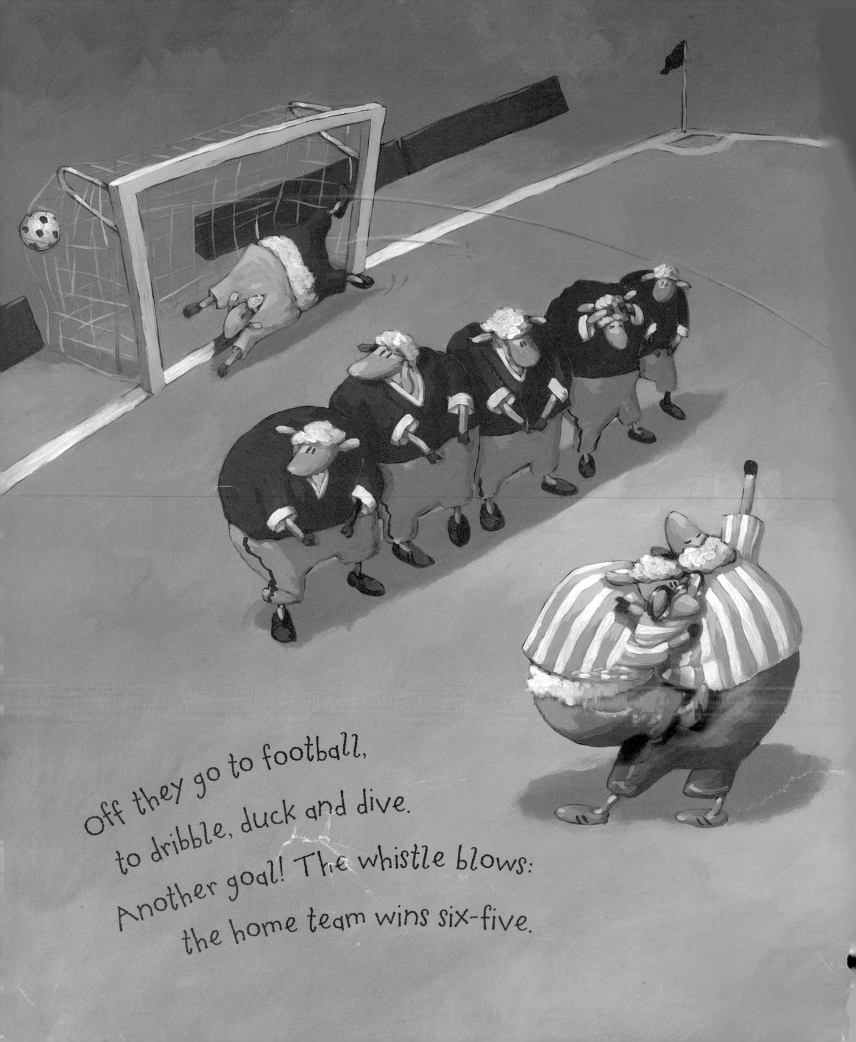

Off they go to football,
to dribble, duck and dive.
Another goal! The whistle blows:
the home team wins six-five.

"Stop!" shouts Phoebe. "Stop it now!
I'm still wide awake!"
But Phoebe's sheep are boiling hot,
and flocking to the lake.

With double flips and somersaults,
into the lake they leap.
One by one, splish splash splosh,
Phoebe counts her sheep!

At last poor Phoebe's quiet.
She doesn't make a peep.
Her eyes are closed, she's nodded off.
Phoebe is asleep!

"Result!" cheer Phoebe's naughty sheep.
Their night has just begun.
"We'd best be on our way," they say.
"It's time we had some FUN!"